ICE AGE 2™
THE MELTDOWN
A MAMMOTH MIX-UP

WRITTEN BY CATHERINE HAPKA
ILLUSTRATIONS BY ARTFUL DOODLERS, UK

HarperKidsEntertainment
An Imprint of HarperCollinsPublishers

ICE AGE 2: A MAMMOTH MIX-UP

Ice Age 2 The Meltdown ™ & © 2006 Twentieth Century Fox Film Corporation. All rights reserved.

HarperCollins®, ≜®, and HarperKidsEntertainment™
are trademarks of HarperCollins Publishers.
Printed in the U.S.A.
For information address HarperCollins Children's Books, a division of HarperCollins Publishers,
1350 Avenue of the Americas, New York, NY 10019.
Library of Congress catalog card number: 2005928972
www.harperchildrens.com
www.iceage2.com
❖
First Edition

Manny was afraid he was
the last mammoth on earth.

Then one day . . . a miracle happened! He met a mammoth named Ellie.

The trouble was, Ellie didn't
know she was a mammoth.

She thought she was a possum.

Ellie introduced Manny to her possum brothers, Crash and Eddie.

"I don't think her tree goes all the way to the top branch," Manny's friend Sid muttered.

Even so, Sid invited Ellie and her brothers to travel with them to the other end of the valley. The ice all around them was melting and they needed to get to higher ground.

"Why did you invite *them*?" Manny demanded. "Because you might be the only two mammoths left on earth!" Sid replied.

As they walked, Manny and Ellie talked.

Manny wondered if he could
ever get through to her.
"Ellie," he said. "Look at our footprints."

Ellie was suspicious.
"How do I know those aren't yours?"

Manny tried again.
"Look at our shadows," he said.

Eventually the group
reached a high rock wall.
There was just one opening.

When Manny led them through,
they found themselves in a beautiful meadow.
It was the Sacred Mammoth Grounds!

Manny and Ellie wandered among
the spirits of past mammoths.

"They're magnificent!" Ellie said in awe.
"So noble and kind. I feel like one of them."

She took a deep breath as she finally realized the truth. "I'm a mammoth!" Manny was thrilled. He wasn't alone in the world anymore.